5

Minute

Stories

DISNEY PRESS

Los Angeles • New York

Published by Disney Press, an imprint of Buena Vista Books, Inc. No part of this book may be reproduced or transmitted in any form or by any means, electronic or mechanical, including photocopying, recording, or by any information storage and retrieval system, without written permission from the publisher.

For information address Disney Press, 1200 Grand Central Avenue, Glendale, California 91201.

Printed in the United States of America

First Hardcover Edition, September 2020

Library of Congress Control Number: 2019919393

1 3 5 7 9 10 8 6 4 2

ISBN 978-1-368-05537-6   FAC-038091-20227

For more Disney Press fun, visit www.disneybooks.com

Contents

Undercover Princess

Mira is a little girl with a big job: royal detective! She helps people all around her city, Jalpur, by solving mysteries. One sunny morning, Mira gets called to the palace by Queen Shanti. The queen must have a new case for her! Mira's mongoose friends, Mikku and Chikku, go along.

"Birdie want a snack?" Chikku asks a colorful bird.

"Birdie want a snack?" the bird repeats. Mira explains that this is a myna bird. It repeats things people say.

Queen Shanti tells Mira that the bird heard some troubling news. The bird repeats what it overheard someone say: "We're going to steal the Gem of Jalpur at the royal party tonight!"

"We can't let that happen!" says Mira. "I'm on the case! How can I help, Your Majesty?"

The queen asks Mira to come to the royal party and stay on the lookout for anyone who tries to steal the gem. "But I think you should blend in with the guests," says the queen. "I would like you to go undercover . . . as a princess!"

Mira is surprised. She's not sure how to act like a princess. Queen Shanti tells her not to worry. Prince Neel will give her royal training.

Prince Neel and his older brother, Prince Veer, meet Mira at her house. Mira has to stand up straight, wear a lot of heavy jewelry, and walk and talk like a princess. It is hard work!

After a lot of practice, Neel and Veer think Mira is finally ready. Mira gets a new princess dress and a secret identity. "It is my pleasure to introduce . . . Princess Heera!" Neel announces.

Mira isn't the only one going undercover. Her cousin, Priya, is assisting Princess Heera in a lady-in-waiting disguise. And Mikku and Chikku are dressed as royal food servers!

"We're happy to help," says Mikku, "especially if we get to be near the snacks!"

Mira arrives at the royal party in disguise. Kings, queens, princes, and princesses watch her enter the palace. No one has even seen this princess before!

"Hello, Princess Heera," Queen Shanti says with a wink. Then she whispers, "Good luck finding the thieves, Mira!"

Mira goes to check on the Gem of Jalpur. "The gem is exactly where it should be," she says.

"So far, so good!" says Priya.

"Hey, I found the thief!" says Mikku. "It's Chikku! He just stole one of my snacks."

Mira laughs and reminds them to be on the lookout for anyone trying to steal the *gem*—not the food.

Two musicians begin to play. They leave the stage and walk through the party guests with their instruments. Suddenly, one of them trips and falls over. "Oops!" she says. "I'm so clumsy!" Everyone turns to look as a royal guard rushes over and helps her up.

In the commotion, Mira realizes no one is guarding the Gem of Jalpur.

Mira and her friends rush back to the glass case. They are relieved to find the gem inside. But Mira notices something strange. "Isn't the Gem of Jalpur blue?" Neel nods. It is.

"Then we have a big problem," says Mira, "because this gem is green!" Mira goes to tell the queen that the Gem of Jalpur has been replaced with a fake. Queen Shanti tells Mira that she believes in her and knows she will find the real gem.

Mira and her friends check the crime scene for clues.
Mira finds a red tassel on the floor.

She thinks maybe whoever stole the gem has red tassels on their clothing. Mira tells her friends to spread out and look for more.

Mikku and Chikku find one on a tray of desserts they served to the musicians.

Mira uses her spyglass to find one on the stage.

"It looks like the same person who was near the gem also took a dessert from Mikku and Chikku and was on the stage," says Mira.

"Let's think this through!" Mira says. "We found red tassels in three places: by the gem case, on the food tray, and on the stage. And there are only two people who were in all three of these places: the musicians who were playing in the crowd. And their instruments have red tassels on them! We need to talk to them."

Mira finds the musicians, but they run out the palace door before she can ask them questions.

Mira calls for backup. "Deputy Oosha, stop them!" she cries. The police cow steps out in front of the musicians, blocking their path. "Moooooo!"

Mira and her friends run up to the musicians. "Excuse me," Mira says, "did you steal the Gem of Jalpur?"

"Of course not!" says the drummer. "Besides, if I did steal it, where is it now?"

Mira points to the blue gem in his turban. "Right there. Your friend pretended to trip so everyone would be distracted. Then, when no one was looking, you replaced the blue Gem of Jalpur with the fake green one."

Case closed.

Mira hands the gem to Queen Shanti.

"Brilliant job, Mira," says the queen. "I knew you would solve this case. Deputy Oosha, take them away."

"Mooo!" says Deputy Oosha.

Now that the gem has been returned to Queen Shanti, she puts it on and shows it to her guests. "Ladies and gentlemen, I'm happy to present the Royal Gem of Jalpur!"

Everyone at the party is amazed by the beautiful precious stone.

Queen Shanti asks Mira to get up onstage with her. "Earlier tonight, two thieves tried to steal the gem," the queen says. "But they didn't get away with it, thanks to our royal detective, Mira!"

Everyone in the crowd gasps. They had no idea that Princess Heera was really the royal detective of Jalpur.

Hooray for Mira! She solved the case again.

Adventures in Puppy-Sitting

One morning, Bob wakes up the puppies with some good news. "Morning, sleepy-snouts! Guess what? My friend just got a new puppy named Baby."

Baby? Bingo and Rolly think that is a funny name for a puppy!

"She doesn't want the puppy to get lonely while she's at work, so I said Baby can stay here with you today, and you can keep her company!"

The pups think that is a great idea!

As soon as Bob leaves to get Baby, Bingo looks at Rolly. "Let's get ready!" Their mission: to be the best puppy-sitters ever!

Bingo points out that great puppy-sitters always have food ready.

Rolly agrees. "So let's give Baby her own dish. You know, to help her feel at home."

Bingo finds a small teacup to use as Baby's bowl. "If we each share a few of our kibbles, that'll fill it up."

Rolly adds some kibble to the teacup. "Bow and wow!"

Rolly looks at his brother. "What else do great puppy-sitters do?"

"They're good at making sure puppies get naps. We need to find a spot for Baby's nap time."

From the bookshelf, Hissy chimes in. "Baby could sleep in one of Bob's shoes. That's what you two goofballs used to do."

Rolly smiles as he remembers sleeping in Loafy, Bob's old loafer shoe. The puppies go searching for it.

In Bob's closet, they burrow through a pile of Bob's shoes.

Rolly pulls out the oldest, rattiest one. "Loafy! My old sleeping shoe! And I still fit . . . sort of. . . . Not really."

The pups are sure that Baby will love sleeping in Loafy . . . just as soon as Rolly can get out of it.

Next they decide to gather some toys for Baby to play with. Bingo's eyes grow wide. He knows the perfect toy for Baby to play with. "Mr. Mousey! I haven't seen that squeaky toy in forever!"

The pups run to find Mr. Mousey. It's old and worn, and it's missing its nose. But the puppies know Baby will still love it!

Just then, the puppies hear the front door open. They run over, excited to meet little Baby.

Bob stands in the doorway, holding on to a leash. "Come on in, Baby." Hissy and the pups get a great big surprise. Little Baby is a gigantic Great Dane puppy!

After Bob leaves for work, Baby starts whimpering and crying.

But Bingo and Rolly know just what to do to make the puppy feel better. "Don't worry, Baby. It's our mission to be the greatest puppy-sitters ever!"

Bingo nudges Mr. Mousey toward her. Baby grabs the squeaky toy. Her tail wags excitedly . . . and she's off! She happily throws Mr. Mousey in the air and then runs after it, knocking over everything in her path. Soon the whole room is a complete mess!

Rolly realizes they have to find something else for Baby to do before the living room gets completely ruined. "I know what I always want to do: eat!"

The pups lead Baby into the kitchen and offer her the small teacup of food. But Baby devours her food in one bite . . . and then eats both bowls of the pups' food, too!

Bingo looks at Rolly. "We'd better get Baby outside before she destroys the house!"

In the backyard, Bingo and Rolly decide to teach Baby some games. Bingo picks up a stick. "This is called fetch. I throw the stick, and Rolly brings it back." Bingo throws the stick across the yard. Rolly runs back and drops the stick in front of Baby.

"Now it's your turn, Baby!" Bingo throws the stick again.

Instead of fetching the stick, Baby comes back with an entire tree. Rolly worries Baby might destroy the whole yard.

"Let's take the puppy to the dog park!" Bingo suggests. A.R.F. looks at the mess in the backyard. He can't wait to clean it up!

At the dog park, Baby runs around excitedly as Bingo and Rolly show her all the neat stuff there is to do.

Bingo watches her explore. "Baby sure seems happy!"

"Look at us being great puppy-sitters!" Rolly says.

Baby spots a squeaky stuffed toy across the park! Joyfully, she runs over and picks it up.

But the squeaky toy belongs to Cupcake. "That's mine!"

Cupcake grabs the other end of the toy and pulls. Baby playfully tugs back . . . until Cupcake narrows her eyes and growls.

Baby lets go. Baby's eyes brighten, and she runs off without looking back.

Meanwhile, Bingo and Rolly are returning a stick to its owner. "Now *that's* how you play fetch, Baby." Bingo turns to find her, but she is gone! The pups look all around the dog park, but Baby is nowhere to be seen!

Cupcake walks over to them. "Are you looking for that big drooly puppy that tried to take my squeaky toy before she ran outta here?"

Rolly nods. "Which way did she go?"

Cupcake just shakes her head.
"Only you two could lose the
biggest puppy in the dog park."

Then it strikes Bingo: "She is the biggest! Rolly, we just have to follow the biggest paw prints."

Rolly looks down and spots a large paw print in the dirt. "Like this one?"

"Exactly like that one!" Bingo looks around and finds a whole trail of big paw prints. "Follow those paw prints! Thanks, Cupcake!"

Bingo and Rolly follow the paw prints out of the park. Then they follow the trail of prints and slobber through the neighborhood until they realize they are headed straight for their house.

Bingo stops suddenly. "Rolly! I think I figured it out. Baby was trying to play with Cupcake's squeaky toy right before she ran off."

"She's going back to our house for Mr. Mousey!" Rolly says.

Back at the house, the pups are delighted to find Hissy playing fetch with Baby and Mr. Mousey.

Bingo smiles at his brother. "High paw, Rolly!"

"High paw, Bingo!"

Hissy stops when she sees the pups. "I've got to admit it is kind of fun to have a puppy around to play this game."

Rolly grins. "You know, we're still puppies, too."

"I mean, we're still a little bit little," Bingo says.

Hissy shrugs. "Then get in this game. There's room for two more!"

"Yes!" Rolly says.

Later, when Bob gets home, the house is quiet. He finds all the animals snuggled up together.

Bob smiles at Bingo and Rolly. "Wow! The puppy really tuckered you out, huh?" The pups sleepily open their eyes. "Looks like you guys ended up being great puppy-sitters."

Going Batty

Vampirina Hauntley is excited! Her family just moved from Transylvania to Pennsylvania. They're a little bit different from the other families in the neighborhood. That's because Vampirina and her family are vampires.

Vampirina unpacks the last box of cobwebs.

"It sure looks spooky in here," she says. "It feels like home."

Now that they're all settled in, Vee is excited to make new friends. Her friends Demi the ghost and Gregoria the gargoyle came with them from Transylvania, but Vee wants to make some human friends, too.

"Just remember that sometimes humans can be a little jumpy," says Vee's mom, Oxana. Her parents explain that people are sometimes scared of things they haven't seen before.

Just then, the doorbell shrieks. It's their neighbor Edna. She welcomes the Hauntleys to the neighborhood with a yummy plate of cookies.

But when Edna walks inside, she gets a bit of a surprise. "The statue! It moved!" Edna cries.

Then she bumps into Penelope, Vampirina's pet plant. Penelope opens her mouth wide. Edna screams, flinging her plate of cookies into the air. Edna is so spooked she runs right out the door.

"Uh-oh," Vee says. "Humans *are* jumpy." Now Vee is worried that making new friends will be harder than she thought. And when Vee gets worried, she gets the battys!

"Don't worry," says Oxana. "All vampires get the battys when they're nervous."

Vee looks down. "But I'm scared I won't make any friends in Pennsylvania."

"Of course you'll make friends," says Oxana.

"But you won't make them in here," adds her dad, Boris. "So why not go outside and play?"

Vampirina and Demi go outside to play. "Let's show the human world how lovable you are," says Demi.

Just then, Vee spots the kids next door. "Demi, hide!" she whispers. Demi quickly darts behind a tree so he won't spook them.

The boy points to Vee's house. "It's totally haunted!" he says. "No, it's not," the girl insists, rolling her eyes. Then she spots Vampirina. "I know! Let's ask her!"

The kids walk to the fence. "Hi, I'm Poppy. And this is my brother, Edgar."

"I'm Vampirina. I just moved in!" says Vee with a smile.

"My brother thinks your house is haunted!" Poppy says. "So why don't you invite us over to prove that it's not?"

Vee can't believe her neighbors want to come over to play! But when Vee opens the front door, it makes a big creak!

"Hear that?" says Edgar. "That is classic haunted house!"

Vee takes Poppy and Edgar to her room and shows them her favorite dolls from Transylvania.

"This is Ghastly Gayle," says Vee. "And I love Creepy Caroline. She wears her hair in serpent braids." Poppy thinks Vee's dolls are different—and really fun.

But Edgar doesn't want to play with dolls. He wants to see something spooky, so he leaves.

Thinking the humans are gone, Demi pops through the wall. "Hi, Vee!" But then he spots Poppy.

"Ghost!" Poppy shrieks.

"Human!" Demi shouts.

"Oh, no!" says Vee, getting another case of the battys.

"Ah! Bat!" shouts Poppy.

"It's just me, Vampirina!" Vee says quickly. "I didn't mean to scare you."

Poppy is startled—and a little confused. "You're . . . a bat?"

"Sometimes. Not always," says Vee. "But it is kinda fun to fly." She swoops and soars around the room.

Poppy smiles. Having a friend who can turn into a bat might be kind of neat!

Just then, Edgar comes back. He heard Poppy scream. "Is it a one-eyed goblin? Or a mummy in the closet?" asks Edgar excitedly.

Before Edgar sees her as a bat, Vee turns back into a girl. "You can tell him, Poppy," she says quietly.

"Oh, that was nothing," says Poppy. "I screamed because . . . Vee and I both love Justin Teether and the Singing Sirens!"

"Awww, man!" Edgar says, disappointed. "Call me if something spooky happens. I'm out!"

"So, you still want to be my friend?" asks Vee.

Poppy shrugs. "I wanted to be your friend before you turned into a bat, so why wouldn't I want to be your friend afterwards, too?"

Vampirina smiles and then gives her new friend a big hug. It looks like making friends in Pennsylvania isn't so scary after all.

One Unicorny Day

Penelope Pony is having a great day at the Longtree Horse Ranch. Lisa is busy tending to the other animals when Penelope spots a butterfly. Suddenly, Penelope is running out of the ranch.

Penelope chases the butterfly off the ranch, over a hill, and into Mickey's garage. She gallops past Goofy, who is testing out his new cotton candy maker.

"Yummers!" says Goofy.

"*Neigh!*" whinnies Penelope.

Crash goes the cart. *Splat* goes the pretty pink cotton candy—right on Penelope's head!

Penelope follows the butterfly into Minnie's makeover salon.

Before she knows it, she is getting a makeover herself!

A bit of glitter here . . .

A little paint there . . .

Penelope gets made over mane to tail.

She looks like a pretty, sparkly, magical unicorn!

Penelope trots around, following the beautiful butterfly. She has never seen anything like it before. She chases it past Pluto's doghouse.

And then she just about catches the butterfly while she is running by Clarabelle's house. Clarabelle is shocked.

In her excitement, Clarabelle calls Daisy. "I just saw a unicorn on my street!"

Daisy gasps. "I love unicorns!" she exclaims. "I'll be right there!"

Daisy rushes over to her friends. "Clarabelle saw a unicorn run past her house!" she says.

"Phooey!" Donald huffs. "There's no such thing as unicorns." He crosses his arms and looks at Mickey. Mickey and Goofy both shrug.

"Just because you've never seen one doesn't mean they aren't real," Daisy tells Donald. She drives to Clarabelle's as fast as she can.

Just then, Mickey gets a phone call. It is Lisa from the Longtree Horse Ranch.

"Hi, Mickey. My pony Penelope wandered off. Could you help me round her up?"

"Sure thing," Mickey replies. "Saddle up, everybody!" Mickey tells the gang about the missing pony.

"Wait a minute," Minnie says to herself. "A missing pony *and* a unicorn sighting on the very same day?"

Daisy pulls up in front of Clarabelle's house. "Which way did it go?" Daisy asks.

Clarabelle points down the road, and Daisy zooms off right away.

Daisy drives until she sees a trail of glittery horseshoe prints. "The unicorn can't be far!" she squeals.

Daisy is excited. She follows the trail of horseshoes as far as she can.

Meanwhile, Donald is driving downtown when he spots a pony. He twirls his lasso and ropes it.

"Gotcha, Penelope!" he shouts. He pulls on his rope and stops his car just beside the horse. He is very proud of himself for being the one to wrangle the pony.

But when Donald finally catches up with the pony, he sees that it isn't Penelope after all. It is just two people dressed up as a pony for a costume party.

Donald is furious and begins yelling at the two partygoers. And he is wondering where Penelope can be and if he is ever going to find her.

Just then, Penelope trots past them. She is still following the butterfly. Donald's jaw drops to the ground.

"The unicorn is real?" Donald sputters. "I can't believe it . . . but I saw it with my own two eyes!"

Donald sees Minnie drive by. He waves her down. "Minnie! I just saw the unicorn!" he shouts.

"Are you sure?" Minnie asks.

"I'm sure! I'm sure," Donald replies. "Look! There's unicorn dust on my bumper."

Minnie takes a closer look and giggles. "Donald, that's not unicorn dust," she says. "It's paint from my makeover salon. I'd recognize it anywhere!"

Not far away, as Daisy drives past the park, she sees something glittery and sparkly in the sunlight. "The unicorn's over there!" she cries.

Daisy speeds over to where she saw the unicorn. Carefully, she goes to investigate what is in the bushes. She is sure to move slowly so she won't spook the unicorn. After all, Daisy has spent all this time looking for it. She doesn't want it running away.

Mickey, Minnie, Donald, and Goofy arrive just in time to see Penelope step out from the bushes.

"Hot dog!" Mickey shouts. "The unicorn is real!"

"Gawrsh!" Goofy guffaws. "A unicorny!"

Goofy accidentally bumps his head against the Tubster's plumbing. Water blasts from the showerhead, and Penelope prances into the spray.

"The unicorn is a . . . pony?" Daisy says in disbelief.

"I'm sorry, Daisy," Minnie says. "Penelope wandered off the ranch and got into my makeover salon. She must have gotten spray-painted, and everyone thought she was a unicorn."

"Well, she might not be real, but that doesn't mean there aren't real unicorns out there somewhere!" Daisy insists.

Lisa comes to pick up Penelope and take her back to the ranch. She thanks everyone for their help in finding Penelope. "I hope she didn't cause too much trouble today," Lisa says.

The friends wave goodbye to Lisa and Penelope.

As Lisa and Penelope drive away, Daisy is distracted by something on a hill just through the park. She points and gets very excited. Donald looks at what she is pointing at and shakes his head. "Magical!" Daisy says with a happy sigh. "I knew they were real!"

Toy Hospital

Doc McStuffins is ready for a new adventure! Grandma gave her a magical present. It's called a Toy-Sponder. It will take Doc and her toys to a brand-new place. All Doc has to do is push the button!

The brand-new place is called
McStuffinsville. It's a totally terrific
toy town! The McStuffins Toy
Hospital is at the center of it all.

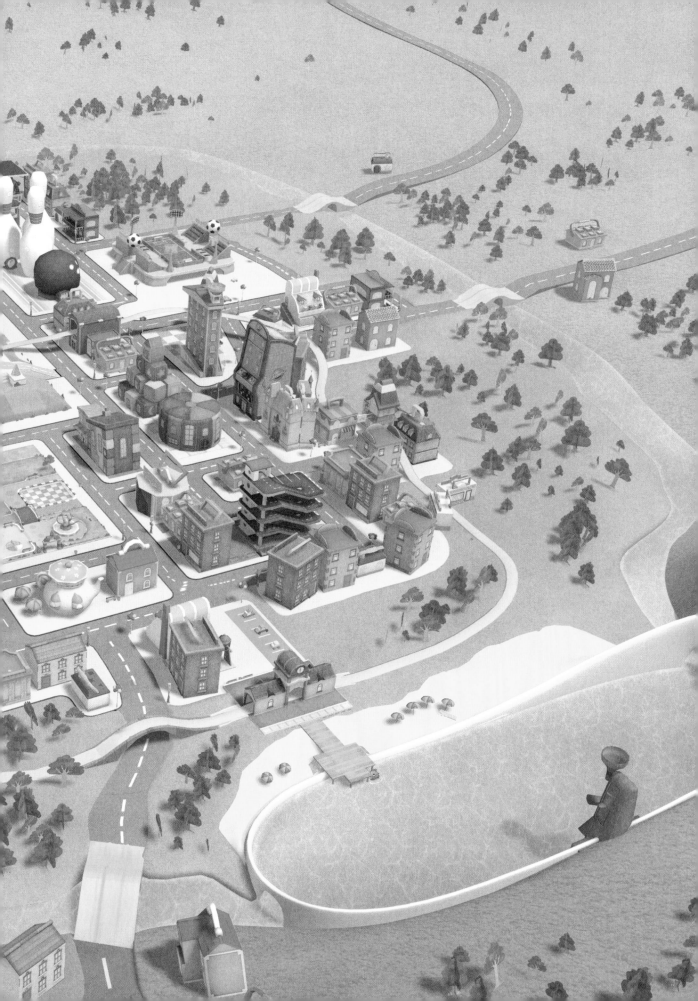

The Toy-Sponder takes them to McStuffins Toy Hospital. Grandma McStuffins has another present. It's a doctor's coat—perfect for the chief resident of McStuffins Toy Hospital. She knows it's the perfect job for Doc.

Doc's toys can't wait to explore the toy town.

"We can check out the town later," Doc tells the toys. "But right now, there are toys to fix here in the Toy Hospital. Come on!"

The halls of the hospital are hustling and bustling. Doctors, nurses, and orderlies are busy with hospital business. Hallie admires the fancy hospital equipment.

"Thank the feathery heavens you're here!" Professor Hootsburgh says. So many toys need fixing . . . too many for Doc to fix alone!

"With the right training, my toys could help me," Doc says. So she asks Professor Hootsburgh to teach the Toy Hospital's first medical school class.

Hallie looks around the emergency room and says, "This place is busier than a bunch of bumblebees at a buttercup bazaar!"

The hospital is a lot bigger than Doc's clinic, but Doc believes in her toy team! Professor Hootsburgh quickly gives them a lesson in making a diagnosis. "One toy at a time," Doc tells them.

Doc and Hallie get to work immediately. There are so many toys in need here! But she has a lot of help from her own toys.

Get-Well Gus delivers gifts and cards to patients at the hospital. He has made so many toys feel better! But now he has crashed and lost one of his wings. Doc and Hallie head to the operating room to give Gus a new wing that can act just like his original one—a prosthetic wing!

Now it's time to choose a perfect get-well gift for Gus at the hospital gift shop!

Hallie picks up a picture book and thinks that might be the perfect gift. Lambie is over by the flowers. She thinks that the colors will brighten up Gus's room and make him happy. Stuffy has picked out a very funny card that he knows will make Gus laugh. Chilly believes chocolate is the best get-well gift of all. Doc thinks these are some great get-well gifts.

When it comes to fixing toys, practice makes perfect. So the medical students head to the sewing and stuffing room to work on their skills.

Chilly is very nervous he might hurt the teddy bear. Doc assures him it doesn't hurt the bears one bit!

In the hospital nursery, it's plain to see that one student has a knack for a special job. Lambie is right at home cuddling baby dolls!

She practices giving the baby dolls their bottles and swaddling them into their cribs.

Stuffy isn't sure where he fits in at the hospital until he visits the Pet Vet Center. It turns out he has a special way with all the toy pets!

At the end of the day, it's time for rounds. That's when Doc and the toys go all around the hospital to check on the patients they treated earlier.

Doc is happy to see her patients in good spirits. She is very proud of herself and the rest of her toys for having such a great day!

A Rainy-Day Adventure

One day, all the friends are together in the Clubhouse to meet Daisy's new kitten. Suddenly, a clap of thunder shakes the Clubhouse. The kitten tries to meow, but it comes out as a squeak. "I'll name her Squeaky!" says Daisy. Everyone laughs.

"Aw, phooey, I didn't know it was going to rain this afternoon. Now we'll be stuck indoors with nothing to do," Donald says.

"There must be lots of things we can do right here in the Clubhouse!" Mickey says.

"So what exactly is there to do?" asks Daisy. The friends all hear a tapping sound.

"Oh, pickle juice!" says Donald. "What we're hearing is water dripping through a leak in the roof!" But as the friends look up, they can see it is four leaks in the roof.

The friends use the four ceramic frogs they have around the Clubhouse to catch all the drops of water.

"It had better stop raining before these frogs' bellies get full!" Donald says.

"Speaking of bellies," says Goofy, patting his tummy, "let's go to the kitchen and get a snack."

"Eureka!" says Mickey. "We have our next project!"

Everyone hurries to the kitchen. Dirty bowls and baking trays are
everywhere. The friends won't be able to make a snack in this dirty
kitchen. It looks like they have something else to do: clean the kitchen!
Donald carries dirty dishes to the sink. Minnie wipes the counters.
Daisy puts away ingredients. Mickey turns on the water to start
washing a mountain of dishes. And Goofy pours dishwashing soap
into the sink.

Pop! Pop! Pop! Pluto chases and bites into the bubbles.

"Say, Goofy," says Mickey, "how about you dry the dishes?"

"Sure thing!" says Goofy, waving soap bubbles away from his face. Two soap bubbles float into his eyes. Goofy closes his eyes and reaches for a dishtowel. But he picks up Squeaky by mistake.

Goofy opens his eyes. "Well, I'll be!" he says. "You know, that towel didn't feel right." He puts Squeaky down.

Squeaky shakes her little body to get the water off her fur. She sprinkles drops of water onto Pluto. Pluto barks.

"Gee, with all the rain and the water from washing dishes, it feels like we've had a boatload of water today!" says Mickey.

"Being on a boat would be fun," says Goofy.

"Like a pirate ship!" says Minnie.

"Let's be pirates!" says Donald.

They all pick up striped napkins to wear, and they look like pirates. "Let's head for the high seas, mateys!" says Daisy. Everyone smiles and claps their hands in excitement. But then they look at each other. "Um, what exactly does that mean?" asks Minnie.

They all run up to the bathtub and grab a toy pirate ship. Everyone takes a turn sailing the toy pirate ship back and forth—except for Squeaky and Pluto. They've had enough water for the day.

"We're sailing through the high seas, looking for buried treasure!" says Donald.

Mickey finds some gold coins with the friends' faces on them. "I'm going to hide these throughout the Clubhouse, and each one of you has to find your coin and bring it back. The one who finds their own coin and the coin with my face on it wins!" says Mickey.

"What do we win?" asks Daisy.

Mickey thinks for a minute. "The bouquet of flowers in the living room," he says.

Donald finds his coin in the soap dish in the bathroom. Daisy finds her coin in the potted plant in the reading room. Goofy finds his coin on the deck of the toy pirate ship. Minnie finds her coin on a pillow in the den. Pluto finds his coin right next to the Mousekedoer. And Squeaky finds her coin in the linen closet. But she takes a catnap on the soft towels.

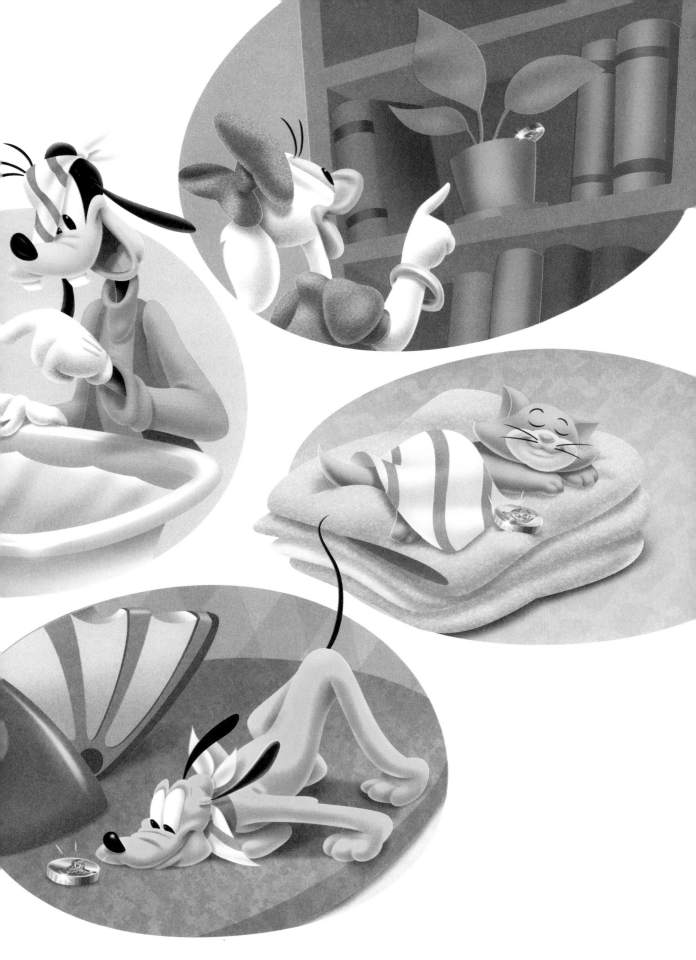

"Did everyone find the right coin?" Mickey asks when they are all together again.

Everyone holds up a coin. "Good job!" says Mickey. "But did anyone find the coin with my face on it?"

They all shake their heads.

Mickey laughs. "I knew that!" he says. "That's because I hid the coin where no one would ever think to look. My pocket!" Mickey pulls out the coin. Everyone laughs.

"Let's drink root beer and eat popcorn to celebrate a great day!"
says Mickey.

"Who cares about the rain!" says Daisy. "We pirates know how to
have fun no matter where we are!"

"Arr! You said it, matey!" says Donald. Pluto barks.

Mickey passes around the popcorn. "What a great day we had here
in the Clubhouse!" he says. The friends had so much fun. And no one
even realized the rain had stopped.

Father's Day Countdown

Bingo and Rolly are visiting their friend Keia at her doghouse for a day of fun. They are in her craft room when they decide to try out their flying machines. The pups are hooked up and ready to go when . . . *crash!*

They end up completely tangled in the yarn.

"How bad is it, Keia?" Bingo asks nervously.

"Looks preeetty tangly," she responds.

"Nothing's too tangly for Keia, master untangler!" Rolly says.

"Hmmm . . . let's see. Over, then under," Keia says to herself, concentrating.

Luckily, Keia manages to untie them. They wiggle free, and the three pups race to the yard to find Chloe.

"Hey, you guys!" Chloe says excitedly, doing a pirouette. "Check out my shoes! It's Father's Day, and my daddy's flying home from a business trip in Saint Louis just in time to take me to a father-daughter dance!" She can hardly wait for her dad to get home.

Just then, her mom comes out, holding her cell phone. Chloe's dad is on the line.

Chloe runs to the phone to talk to her dad. "Happy Father's Day, Daddy!" she says. "Are you at the airport?"

"Bad news, Chloe-bear . . ." her dad begins. "The plane's broken, so I may not make it to the dance. I'm so sorry. I love you."

After they hang up, Chloe turns to her mom with tears in her eyes. "I wish Daddy could get home for the dance."

"Me too," her mom says. "Maybe someone will fix the plane in time."

As soon as Chloe and her mom head inside, the pups decide to come up with a plan.

"We gotta go to Saint Louis to—" Bingo says.

"Fix the plane so Chloe's dad can get to the dance!" Keia finishes.

"Wait for me!" Cagey calls to them. "There's only one thing I love more than this wheel, and that's our Chloe. I want in on this mission!"

The pets all head to the airport to find a plane to Saint Louis. When they get there, they spot Frank and Esther.

"Hustle it, Frank! We gotta catch the plane to Saint Louis!" Esther says.

"That's our ride!" Bingo cheers. "C'mon!"

When they get to the gate, a flight attendant tells Frank and Esther that they've *just* missed the plane. "I'm so sorry," the flight attendant says. "You could take the high-speed train instead."

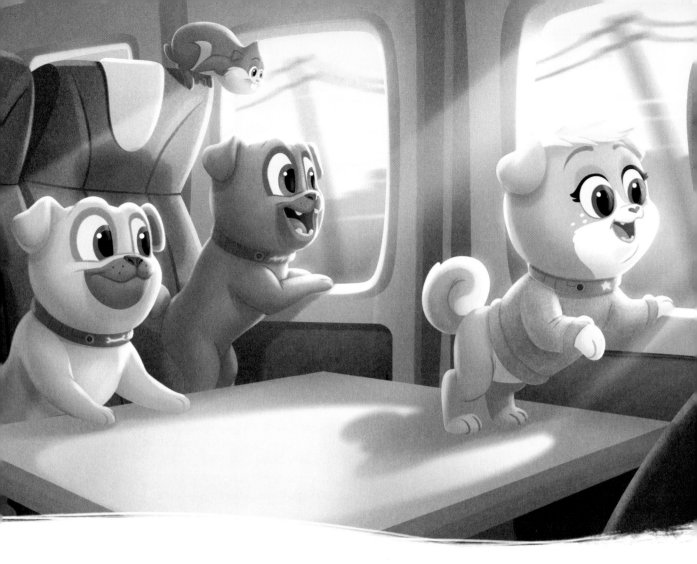

"You heard the lady," Bingo says. "We're taking a train."

"Planes and trains? Ooh! Missions are somethin' else!" says Cagey. "Hey, what's a train?"

Cagey and the pups take the train across the country to Saint Louis. They know they'll need a little luck to get there and bring Chloe's dad back in time for the father-daughter dance.

When the train stops in Saint Louis, the pets hop off with Frank and Esther.

"Which way to Chloe's dad's airport?" Keia asks the pups.

"I dunno," Bingo says.

Suddenly, something catches Bingo's eye. High above, a blimp drifts lazily back and forth.

"We should be able to see Chloe's dad's airport from up there!" says Bingo.

So Bingo, Rolly, and Keia activate their collars, and their helmets and harnesses deploy. Keia then puts a tiny harness on Cagey. They strap in and send their grappling hooks way up to the blimp.

Once they're safely in the blimp, they peer through the blimp door, searching and searching and searching for the . . .

"Airport! There!" Rolly shouts.

"Now we just need to get down there," Rolly says.

"Let's parachute!" Bingo suggests. "Ready, set, jump!"

They push buttons on their collars again, and parachutes deploy.
The pets float down and land in a heap on a spot of grass near
the airport's tarmac.

From the pile, Rolly pulls out a little round gear he was sitting on.

Just then, an airport worker says something about the plane missing a part.

"You found it, Rolly!" says Bingo. "If we can figure out where that gear goes, maybe that will fix the plane."

With the gear, they rush up the stairs to the plane. A tangle of wires pops out from a compartment, covering the space for the missing gear.

"Whoa!" Keia gasps. "That's a lot of wires."

"You're the master untangler, remember?" Rolly adds.

"I believe in you, Sis!" Cagey says. "For Chloe!"

Keia beams and then gets to work, determined to fix the plane.

Keia works quickly to untangle the wires. She clears the way and then clicks the gear into place. The engines fire up! She did it!

"Now Chloe's dad can make it home for the dance," Rolly says.

"And we can make it home if we take the plane, too," says Bingo.

The pets all head inside the airport to search for Chloe's dad. They spot him walking *away* from the gate. He's going to miss the plane unless they find a way to let him know it's taking off soon!

The four friends quickly form a plan. Cagey takes hold of the handle on Chloe's dad's suitcase while Bingo, Rolly, and Keia roll it toward the gate.

Chloe's dad runs after it. The plan is working!

Chloe's dad catches up to his suitcase as he gets to the gate. "I thought the plane was broken!" he says to an airport worker.

"The plane is fixed now and ready for takeoff," the airport worker tells him.

"Yes! He's getting on the plane!" Keia says.

"And so should we!" Rolly reminds them.

When they're back at Keia's house, they run through the doggie door and into the kitchen to find Chloe.

"Wow, look at those dancing shoes!" Chloe's dad says.

"Daddy! You're here!" Chloe cries, running to him for a big hug. "Happy Father's Day, Daddy!"

"I like this whole mission thing," Cagey tells the pups.

MISSION ACCOMPLISHED!

Blooming Bows

It's a busy day at Minnie's Bow-tique. Minnie and Daisy are getting ready for two special visitors.

"Daisy," says Minnie, "did you find the camera?"

"Not yet," replies Daisy. "But I know I have it here somewhere."

Daisy turns around. "Here it is, Daisy," says Minnie.

"Thanks!" says Daisy. "Now I'll be able to get a good picture of you and the twins."

Just then, Minnie hears giggling. "Get ready!" she cries. "Here they come!"

The twins are so excited to show off their costumes to their aunt
Minnie and her friend Daisy. When they burst through the door, they
are wearing their posy petals with big smiles on their faces.

"Ta-daah!" Millie and Melody shout.

"I'm Purple Posy!" says Melody.

"And I'm Rosie Posy!" says Millie.

Minnie greets her twin nieces while Daisy snaps a picture of them.

"Hold that pose, pretty posies!" cries Daisy.

"Oh!" says Minnie.
"You both look simply
adorable!"

As the girls twirl around to show off their costumes, some of the flower petals fall off. Daisy snaps away as Cuckoo-Loca flies in for a closer look.

"All set for the Posy Pageant?" asks Cuckoo-Loca.

"We sure are, Cuckoo-Loca!" says Millie. "Come on, Melody, let's show them our posy prance dance!"

As the girls dance, more and more paper petals fall to the floor.

"Is that supposed to happen?" whispers Cuckoo-Loca, pointing to all the petals on the floor.

"Oh, my," Minnie says.

The twins stare at the petals on the floor.

"Uh-oh," says Melody. "I guess the glue wasn't dry."

"I'll say," says Cuckoo-Loca.

"Don't worry, girls," Minnie says. "We'll fix these right up."

"Oh, please hurry, Aunt Minnie!" says Melody.

"Or else we can't be in the pageant!" cries Millie.

"I've got the sticky-wicky goo-glue!" Daisy cries.

"Good thinking, Daisy!" says Minnie.

Minnie watches as Daisy glues the petals back on. "Let's see, this pink one goes here, this purple one goes there. . . . Wait . . . is that right?" asks Daisy.

"Daisy!" says Melody. "I'm Purple Posy! She's Rosie Posy!"

The girls look at each other and get very sad. Their dance ruined their perfect costumes. What will they do now?

Minnie gives the twins a big hug. "There, there, now, girls," she says. "I'll figure something out."

"But how?" asks Melody. "It's a flower show, not a bow show!"

Suddenly, Minnie has an idea. "Girls!" she calls. "Follow me!"
Grabbing an armful of fabric, Minnie leads the girls to the dressing
room.

While Minnie cuts fabric and ties ribbons, the twins giggle excitedly.
Daisy and Cuckoo-Loca can't wait to see what Minnie is creating.

Soon Minnie reappears.

"Ladies and gentle-bird, introducing our favorite flowers: Rosie Posy and Purple Posy!"

"Pop-up posies!" cries Daisy. "And no glue needed!"

"Now that's what I call getting out of a sticky situation," says Cuckoo-Loca.

"Come on, my little posies," says Minnie. "It's showtime!"

The girls are smiling petal to petal, and they are so happy with their new costumes. Now they are ready for the flower show!

"Hey, girls!" Daisy calls, holding up her camera. "Say posies!"

Millie and Melody wave good-bye as they run out the door.

Minnie, Daisy, and Cuckoo-Loca wave back at the twins, relieved that they could fix their costumes.

"Wow, Minnie!" says Daisy, smiling at her friend. "Who knew you had such flower power?"

"It's like I always say, Daisy," says Minnie. "There's no business like bow business!"

Minnie and Daisy both giggle as they get back to work at the Bow-tique.

Home, Scream Home

Vampirina and her band, the Ghoul Girls, are practicing their new song when Vee's parents walk in. "Vee, do you remember what today is?" Boris asks.

Vee gasps. "Oh my gosh! Today's the Transylvanian Scream Factor competition. It's a contest. Whoever wins is Transylvania's best talent." She explains to her friends.

Oxana announces that they are all going to the Scream Factor competition!

Vee can't wait to show Poppy and Bridget the place where she grew up. Poppy looks down through the fog below. "Wow! Is that . . . Transylvania?"

Vee smiles proudly. "Home, scream home! That's Spookelton Castle! It's where we're going."

After they land their brooms, Vee leads her friends into the castle.
"Come on. We should get backstage," she says.

Backstage, Vee and the girls run into their friends the Scream Girls.
They share hugs all around. Vee smiles. "My dad signed us up to
compete, but I didn't know it was against you guys!"

Just then, another band arrives: Poltergeist Pat and the Boo Boys. As Pat walks past them, he announces that the Scream Girls should get ready to lose. Pat glances at Vee and her friends and shrugs.

He's never heard of the Ghoul Girls, and he declares that a former Transylvanian and a couple of humans can never win Transylvania's top talent show. Then he and the Boo Boys walk off without looking back.

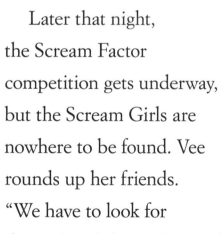

Later that night,
the Scream Factor
competition gets underway,
but the Scream Girls are
nowhere to be found. Vee
rounds up her friends.
"We have to look for
them. Good thing I know this castle like the back of my wings!"

When they reach the Room of Magic Mirrors to ask the magical
reflection ghost, he points to the kitchen, but the Scream Girls aren't
in there.

Vee knows there is only one more place they haven't looked. "The dungeon," she says.

Now Bridget is really spooked. "D-d-dungeon?" When they get there, Gregoria explains that the way into the dungeon is a secret.

Luckily, Vee remembers what to do. "I just have to play an old Transylvanian tune." As Vee hops from one stone to another on the floor, the stones light up and play a spooky melody.

Suddenly, the door to the dungeon opens!

Vampirina leads her friends down the staircase. "Hello? Scream Girls!" she calls out.

At first they don't hear anything, but then . . . "Heeeelp! Heeeelp!"

"It's the Scream Girls!" Vee motions for her friends to follow.

Vee and the gang find Creepy Caroline, Ghastly Gayle, and Franken-Stacey in a dungeon cell. They rush inside . . . and the door slams behind them!

Vee runs to the door . . . and finds Poltergeist Pat! He laughs as he locks them all in and takes the key. Pat says he won't be letting them out until after the show.

Vee is angry. "This isn't winning. This is cheating!" she says. But Poltergeist Pat doesn't care. He'll do anything to sing his way to superstar screamdom.

Vee isn't about to quit. She comes up with a plan. First she transforms into a bat. Demi floats through the door and helps her squeeze through the keyhole. Then, together, they fly off to get the key.

Before long, Vee and Demi spot Poltergeist Pat and the key. But as soon as he sees them headed toward him, he makes the key sprout wings and fly away.

Vee and Demi race after the key, but it is too fast. Just then, Boris sees Vee. When he hears what happened, he springs into action, zipping and zooming through the air until he captures the key.

With no time to lose, Vee and Demi race back to the dungeon and
free their friends. Everyone gathers around Vee to thank her.
"Come on! We gotta go!" Vampirina says.

The Scream Girls rush backstage just in time to hear the announcer introduce them as the final act. Confused, they look at the Ghoul Girls. Vee shrugs. "We're not competing. This is about Transylvanian talent. . . . I don't know how Transylvanian I am anymore."

Vampirina's friends know they have to convince her that she is wrong.

Poppy looks at Vee. "The way you got us around this castle . . . only a Transylvanian could do that."

Franken-Stacey nods. "It's part of who you are. It doesn't matter where you move to. That'll never change."

As the Scream Girls walk onstage, the crowd goes wild!
Franken-Stacey grabs the mic. "Sorry, but tonight is a celebration of
all things Transylvania, and we've got some friends backstage. So give
it up for a spooktacular band: the Ghoul Girls!"

Vee, Poppy, and Bridget look at
each other, shocked. "That's us!" Vee says.
The Ghoul Girls take the stage as Poltergeist Pat
pouts, angry that his plan didn't work.

Bridget, Poppy, and Vampirina rock the house, and the Ghoul Girls become the new Scream Factor champions.

Vee smiles at the crowd. "I guess you can take the ghoul out of Transylvania, but you can't take the Transylvania out of the ghoul!"

Training Daze

"Duck . . . duck . . . duck . . . penguin!" Freddy taps his best buddy, Pip, and runs around the circle of giggling ducklings. The two friends are taking a break from their delivery work to play in the nursery.

But before they know it, playtime is over. The ducklings need to be delivered to their parents!

As Pip and Freddy load up their crate, they see their friend JP, the Super-Duper Flyer, leading three young storks, Jed, Red, and Zed, on a field trip.

"There is a right way and there is a wrong way to deliver babies," says JP. "And I am going to teach you the right way."

JP waves a red flag and tells the young storks to follow it wherever
it goes, no matter what. But before he can start the delivery, JP gets
called away to have his picture taken for *Stork Magazine*.

It's time for Pip and Freddy to deliver their baby ducklings.

"Flamin-gooooooo!" they call. When they take off into the air, the red flag takes off with them!

"Follow the red flag!" says Jed.

"Wherever it goes!" says Red.

"No matter what!" says Zed.

Pip and Freddy are mid-flight when Pip turns around and sees the storks are right behind them! "You should be following JP," Pip tells them.

But the little storks beg to come along with Pip and Freddy on their duckling delivery. Jed pulls out a piece of paper with the instructions JP gave them.

Step 1: Always fly straight when traveling to your destination.

But when Freddy tries to show the little storks how to fly straight, he gets so nervous that he forgets how to fly at all! He does a sideways swoop-de-loop and flies upside down.

Then Freddy loses control and starts falling!

"Hang on, Pip!" cries Freddy.

"Hang on, Pip!" call out Jed, Red, and Zed.

Everyone tumbles to the ground and lands safely. The storks cheer. They're having fun!

Freddy apologizes for the surprise landing. "I just can't fly straight the way it says on JP's instruction sheet."

"It's okay, Freddy," says Pip. "We can walk to the duck pond."

"Follow me!" says Pip. "I'll sniff the way to the pond." The storks check JP's instructions.

Step 2: Always follow the map when navigating to your destination.

"You never follow the map," Freddy whispers to Pip. "You follow your nose!"

But Pip wants to teach the little storks the right way, so he decides to use the map.

Pip leads everyone through the cold and ice, following the map as best he can. "This map has me so confused, I don't even know which way is up," he whispers to Freddy.

Just when Pip and Freddy think this delivery can't get any worse, the ducklings start quacking loudly.

"Poor duckies," says Freddy. "They've been in their crate so long, they're getting cranky!"

"We never should have tried to teach these kids the right way to deliver a baby," Pip says. "We can't even do it ourselves."

Pip feels really bad. He and Freddy only meant to help the young storks. But it seems like they just got them all into trouble. And now the ducklings will not stop crying.

"Sorry, guys," says Pip. "We wanted to show you the right way to deliver a baby, but the truth is, we don't know the right way. We only know our way."

Freddy tries to calm the crate of cranky ducklings with some rocking and humming. They start to giggle.

"Hey, look!" says Jed. "The ducklings really like Freddy's rocking."

"But rocking babies isn't in JP's instructions," says Pip.

"Maybe it doesn't have to be," says Red.

"Freddy didn't fly straight, but he was great at doing a swoop-de-loop!" says Red.

"And, Pip, you knew where we were before you started reading the map!" says Jed.

"What if there's more than one right way to deliver a baby?" says Zed.

"Kids, it's time to put away JP's instructions," says Pip. "We're gonna show you how Pip and Freddy make a delivery!"

Pip and Freddy fly into the air, with Jed, Red, and Zed close behind them. Pip uses his nose to sniff the way. Freddy flaps his wings, doing his best swoop-de-loop.

Finally, they make another landing—but this time it's in the right place.

"And that's how we deliver a baby!" Freddy says proudly.

Back at T.O.T.S., Captain Beakman is impressed.

"But that's not the right way!" JP says.

Captain Beakman shakes her head. "There's more than one right way to deliver a baby," she says. "To another successful delivery for the Junior Fliers!"

Pip and Freddy get a new stamp in their Baby Booklet for taking those ducklings home—their way.

Bingo and Rolly's Birthday

Today is a very special day. The sun is shining, birds are singing, and Bob is sleeping—until Bingo and Rolly leap onto his bed and start to bounce.

"Hooray, it's birthday day!" Rolly shouts.

"Happy birthday, fellas!" Bob lets out a big yawn. "Why don't you play outside until I'm done sleeping?"

The pups run out, laughing all the way. This is going to be the best puppy birthday ever!

Rolly heads straight for his favorite thing in the backyard: a gigantic stack of sticks. "Now that I'm a year older, I'm going to make my stick collection even bigger!" But when he goes to add a new stick to his pile, it topples to the ground. "I wish my sticks would stop spilling everywhere. . . ."

Across the yard, Bingo is playing his favorite game: launching his Captain Dog action figure. He puts the toy into the launcher and hits a button. *BOING!* After chasing it, Bingo reloads the launcher. "Captain Dog to the rescue!" But the spring snaps and Captain Dog goes nowhere. "No! It's broken!" Bingo cries.

"Who's ready for their breakfast birthday bones?" Bob calls.
Bingo and Rolly run inside, thinking breakfast will cheer them up.
Bob promises them a puppy party later. "I made you each a
present. See you tonight!" he says as he leaves for work.

"So, what gifts did you get for each other?" Hissy asks.

Bingo and Rolly are confused. Bob said *he* was giving them presents.

"Don't you want to give something to each other?" Hissy asks.

The puppies exchange looks.

"I want you to have the best birthday ever!" Bingo says to Rolly.

"Ditto!" Rolly replies with his mouth full.

"C'mon, Rolly! We'd better start our gift mission," Bingo says.

Bingo thinks he has found the perfect gift. He runs inside and drops it at Hissy's feet. "I got Rolly a stick from his stick collection," Bingo says.

Hissy laughs. "Why don't you think about something Rolly *doesn't* have?" Bingo thinks for a moment, then remembers what Rolly said earlier. "A stick holder!" Bingo exclaims. He runs off.

Then Rolly comes in with a gift. Hissy laughs again. "That's Bingo's toy," she says.

"That's how I know he'll like it!" Rolly replies.

"What would he like that he doesn't have already?" Hissy asks.

"He used to like launching his Captain Dog fetch toy," Rolly says. "Maybe I can find him something springy!" Rolly dashes out the front door.

Rolly goes to visit their friend Dallie the firehouse Dalmatian. "That spring! It's just what I'm looking for!" Rolly exclaims.

"I'd give it to you, but I need it to prop up the front of my doghouse," Dallie says. "If you've got something else that can get the job done, I'd be happy to trade you."

So Rolly decides to trade his stick collection for Dallie's spring.

"Seems like you really love those sticks, though," says Dallie.

"Yeah," Rolly says, "I do. But not as much as I love my brother! See ya, Dallie. I've got a present to wrap!"

At the dog park, Bingo spots Cupcake and Rufus playing with a box that would be perfect for Rolly's stick collection. He asks if he can give it to Rolly.

"You're barking up the wrong tree," Cupcake says. "Unless . . . you want to trade me something better."

Bingo brings all his favorite toys to Cupcake and Rufus. Cupcake spots Bingo's Captain Dog action figure. "That's the one I want!"

Bingo sighs. "Okay," he says. "For Rolly, I'll trade. He's going to be so excited to see this box!"

The pups bring their presents to the middle of the backyard. "Open yours first!" Bingo shouts.

"No, you go first!" Rolly says.

The brothers open their presents at the same time. "It's a spring to launch your Captain Dog action figure," Rolly says excitedly when Bingo opens his present.

"And yours is a stick holder, for your stick collection!" says Bingo.

"What are you waiting for?" Bingo asks. "Put your sticks in there!"

"The thing is . . . I don't have them anymore. I traded my stick collection to Dallie for that spring," Rolly says. "So let's use it to launch Captain Dog!"

"We can't. . . . I traded Captain Dog to Cupcake for your present," Bingo tells his brother.

"Aren't you sad you can't play with your toys?" Hissy asks.

"Yeah," Bingo says. "But I have a brother who traded his most favorite thing just to make me happy."

"And that's better than any present I can think of," Rolly adds.

A.R.F. thinks this is lovely. "A.R.F. is having big feelings!" he cries.

When Bob gets home, he calls the puppies into the house. "Who's ready for a birthday party?" Bob gives them sweaters he knitted himself.

"We love 'em, Bob!" Bingo says.

"Thank you so much!" Rolly jumps up and down.

A.R.F. is so excited to clean up the party mess, and he starts with the mess the puppies made opening their presents.

Bingo and Rolly's birthday is almost over. But they still have two more presents from Hissy that are waiting in the backyard.

"My stick collection!" Rolly shouts.

"And my Captain Dog! How did you get our stuff back?" Bingo asks.

"I just made a couple of trades," Hissy replies.

Bingo and Rolly give her big puppy hugs. "You're the best kitty sister in the whole world!" Rolly says.

"I know," Hissy says with a smile. "Don't rub it in."

Rolly's stick collection fits perfectly in his new box.

Bingo uses the new spring in his toy launcher and makes the Captain Dog figure fly through the air. "And Captain Dog flies again!" he shouts excitedly.

Hissy watches them play. "Happy birthday, Brothers!"

MISSION ACCOMPLISHED!

Minnie's Vacation Home

One bright cheery morning, Daisy and Cuckoo-Loca are enjoying a healthy breakfast when the phone rings. Minnie quickly picks it up.

"Hello?" Minnie speaks softly, but her roommates can still hear her. "Now, Ms. Mayweather, please promise me that you won't tell my secret."

Minnie hangs up and heads for the door. "Sorry, girls," she says. "I have to go run an errand."

After Minnie leaves, Cuckoo-Loca turns to Daisy. "Something fishy is going on. Let's follow Minnie to see where she's really going."

Daisy agrees. "Let's wear disguises!"

Daisy and Cuckoo-Loca catch up to Minnie as she is driving through Hot Dog Hills.

"She'll never suspect that two fish sellers in a fish truck are following her," Daisy says confidently.

"Hmm," Minnie says. "Now why are two fish sellers in a fish truck following me?" She pulls over and stops.

"Quackers!" Daisy shouts. "Get into fish mode!"

The girls throw open the back doors and pretend to be selling fish. Daisy calls out in a deep voice, "Fresh fish! We've got tuna, cod, squid!"

"They're off the hook!" Cuckoo-Loca adds.

The disguises work. Minnie has no idea that the fish sellers are really her friends. She drives off a minute later, and Daisy and Cuckoo-Loca are not far behind.

Minnie parks in front of a rundown house with a FOR SALE sign in the yard.

The front door opens. "Hello, Minnie," says Ms. Mayweather. "Welcome to your new house!"

Daisy and Cuckoo-Loca can't believe their ears. "This means Minnie is moving out of the apartment!" exclaims Daisy. The girls are heartbroken, but they still want to support their best friend, Minnie.

Inside the house, Minnie walks with Ms. Mayweather. "It'll be so nice to have a place where we can relax on the weekends," she says.

"I bet Daisy and Cuckoo-Loca are excited!" says Ms. Mayweather.

"They will be once I tell them," Minnie says with a giggle. "I wanted to surprise them!"

Just then, Daisy and Cuckoo-Loca knock on the door.

"Your secret's out," Cuckoo-Loca says.

Minnie is relieved. "Oh, good. It's been so hard for me to keep the secret. Come in!"

Daisy and Cuckoo-Loca look around. The house is rundown and badly in need of repair. "It's . . . nice," says Daisy.

"The place needs a lot of fixing up," Minnie admits. "But if we work hard, we can make it look nice again."

"We?" Cuckoo-Loca asks.

"Don't you want to help?" Minnie asks.

Daisy and Cuckoo-Loca don't want to help Minnie move, but they want to be good friends, so they agree.

At the Mixed-Up Motor Lab, Minnie chooses pink paint, curtains, a new rug, and lots of building tools.

Cuckoo-Loca whispers to Daisy, "I can't help Minnie fix this house just so she can move."

Daisy has an idea. "Then we'll *un*-fix the house so she can't move away!"

The tools and supplies are loaded into a nifty Happy Helper Do-It-Yourselfer trailer. "We're ready to fix up the house!" says Minnie.

She is so excited to get to work on the house. She jumps into the driver's seat, ready to go.

"Oh, we're ready, all right," says Daisy. She and Cuckoo-Loca chuckle to each other and exchange winks.

They get in the van with Minnie and she drives away.

The first step to fixing up the house is to replace the old carpet. Minnie and Daisy start at one side and begin to roll it up.

Next Minnie puts down a brand-new carpet. It looks wonderful, but Daisy and Cuckoo-Loca say they are going to make it look even better. They open some paint and draw a picture of themselves.

Minnie pretends to like it. "That rug was too plain anyways," she says.

Minnie decides to paint the living room. She dips her roller into perfectly pink paint. But while she is busy, Daisy pours gray paint into the tray.

Minnie dunks the roller in the paint again. This time, she paints big gray stripes on the wall.

"Yipes, stripes!" she yells.

Daisy smiles. It looks like her plan is working.

Just then, Cuckoo-Loca flies into the kitchen with a bucket of mud. Daisy plans to use it to make a mess.

"This place will be so icky Minnie will never want to move out of our apartment," says Daisy.

But the bucket slips out of Daisy's hand and into the sink. It all gurgles down the drain. When Minnie comes in to clean her paint roller, she turns on the water, and a grimy geyser gushes out of the sink!

"Oh, muddy buttons and bows!" cries Minnie.

Daisy ducks under the sink with a wrench and
stops the mud flow. The kitchen is a mess!
Minnie sighs and says, "Our poor vacation home."

"*Our* vacation home?" Daisy and Cuckoo-Loca say together.

"Yes," says Minnie. "I bought it for us. You said you knew the secret."

Daisy explains that they thought Minnie was moving out of the apartment and leaving them behind.

"Oh, girls," Minnie says with a giggle. "I would never move away from my very best friends. Not never-ever!"

Daisy and Cuckoo-Loca apologize for the trouble they caused.
"Now that we know this is our vacation home, let's really fix it up,"
says Daisy.

"And this time," says Minnie, "no causing messes!"

Suddenly, there is a crack and a rumble. In just seconds, the
whole house collapses around them.

The house is ruined. But on the bright side, the girls can now make it exactly the way they want it to be.

First they need new walls. They hammer boards together and lift the wall frames into place.

After the walls are up, it is time for a new roof. It takes a lot of work to put all the shingles on.

"This place is going to look even better than I expected," says Minnie.

Inside, Daisy installs a new sink and faucet in the kitchen. It works perfectly!

"And no mud!" says Cuckoo-Loca.

"Thank goodness," Minnie says with a laugh.

The finished house is beautiful. It has large rooms, a spiral staircase, huge windows, and an outdoor deck that looks out over the lake.

It is the perfect vacation home.

"I could definitely get used to this," says Cuckoo-Loca.

Minnie and Daisy agree. "I can't wait until we can use it!" Daisy says.

It isn't long before the girls are fully enjoying their lovely vacation home. One afternoon, as the three friends are relaxing on the deck, Minnie's phone rings.

Cuckoo-Loca sits up straight. "Do not answer that!" she insists.

"But why?" asks Minnie.

"Because we're not ready for another house!"